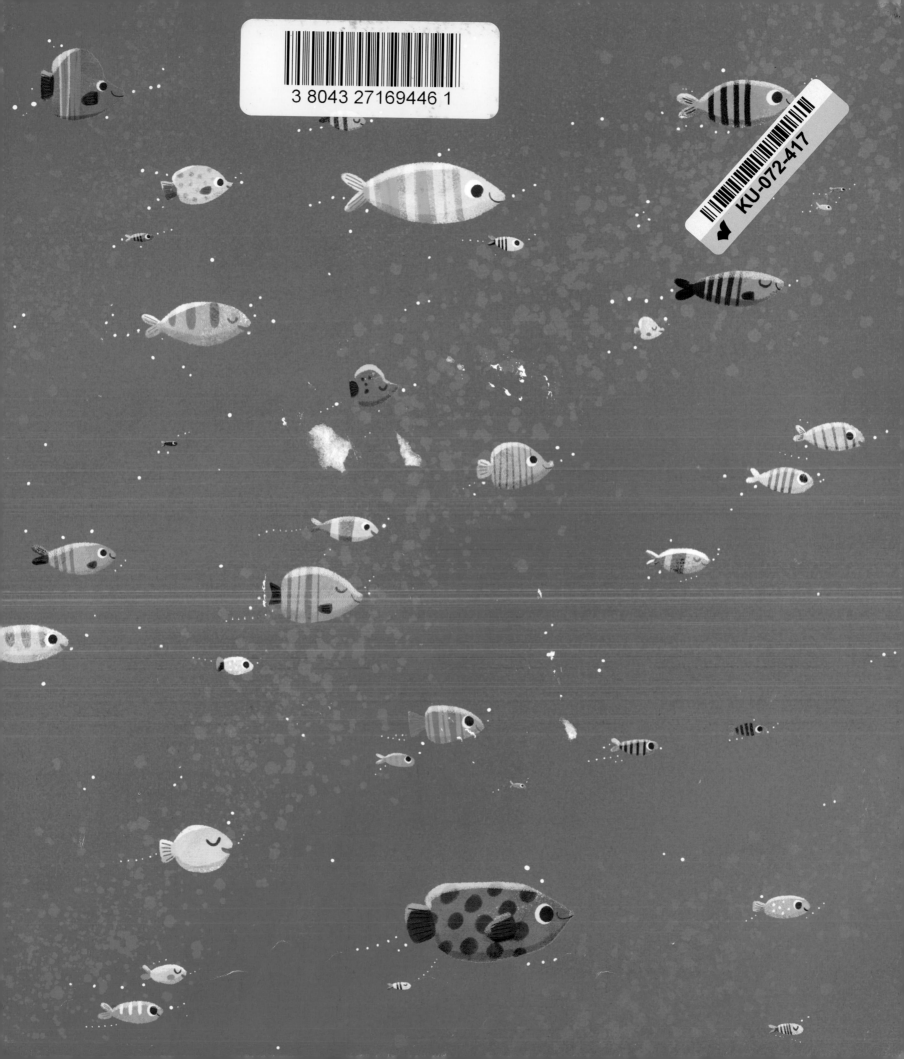

For everyone out there brave
enough to try ~ T C

For Mum and Dad and all
that you do ~ T N

LITTLE TIGER PRESS LTD,
an imprint of the Little Tiger Group
1 Coda Studios,
189 Munster Road,
London SW6 6AW
www.littletiger.co.uk

First published in Great Britain 2020

Text copyright © Tracey Corderoy 2020
Illustrations copyright © Tony Neal 2020
Tracey Corderoy and Tony Neal have asserted their rights
to be identified as the author and illustrator of this work
under the Copyright, Designs and Patents Act, 1988
A CIP catalogue record for this book is available
from the British Library

All rights reserved • ISBN 978-1-78881-586-4
Printed in China • LTP/1400/2941/0919

2 4 6 8 10 9 7 5 3 1

IMPOSSIBLE!

Tracey Corderoy

Tony Neal

LITTLE TIGER
LONDON

On the sunniest street, in the busiest city,
Dog ran a neat little laundry.
He whistled as he washed his customers' clothes
and hung them on the rooftop to dry.

But the city was noisy, even at night.
At bedtime, Dog turned on his cosy ocean nightlight.
It filled his dreams with the soft, gentle swish of the sea.

If only he could visit the real ocean.
But it was just too far away . . .

Instead, Dog made little boats
and read thrilling tales of the sea.

Then one day, he discovered a
brand new washing powder . . .

"Ocean Magic -
for seaside freshness
with every wash!"

He couldn't wait to try it out!

Dog poured in the powder and the clothes began to swirl.

ocean magic

Soon the smell of the seaside filled his flat - the hot sun, the salty waves, the golden sand! "Magical!" Dog smiled. It felt like he was really there.

But that wasn't all.

"A crab?" cried Dog.
"Goodness! That's impossible!"

"Ugh!" groaned the
crab dizzily.
"I feel sick!"

Dog dashed to the rescue with a fresh pot of tea. "However did you get here?" he asked. Crab shrugged. "One minute I was on my beach - then, like magic, I was in your washing machine!"

He gulped down his tea. "Right, home-time!" said Crab. "Can I borrow your bike?" "Of course," agreed Dog. "But will your feet reach the pedals?"

"So, post me instead," tried Crab. "You'd get squashed!" spluttered Dog. "I shall walk, then!" announced Crab, scuttling to the door.

"Wait - it's MILES," gasped Dog. "Look!"
He pointed to a map on the wall and sighed.
"I've always wanted to go to the seaside myself.
But it's too far for me to drive. It's impossible."

"I've got it!" beamed Crab. "Let's drive there TOGETHER. A road trip. It'll be fun!"
"I'm n-not sure," began Dog. But he longed to see the ocean, and to help Crab too.

Dog sat and listened all night to Crab's plans.
"Let's give it a go," he said finally.

Early next day, Dog hopped in the van to deliver his customers' washing. But when he got back his suitcase was all packed and waiting!

Dog gasped. It was one thing to SAY he'd go, but quite another to DO it.

"It's **impossible**," he said sadly. "I can't leave. I'm sorry."

"It's only impossible if you say it is," replied Crab. "Can't we try?"

And so they did!
"We're off!" cheered Dog.
This road trip just might be possible after all.

LEAVE CITY

REALLY HIGH!

Dog and Crab travelled for weeks and weeks. They drove through dark caves, and crossed giant waterfalls. And every day they added special memories to their map.

CAVES

EEK!

RICKETY BRIDGE!!

WOODLAND WALK

DARK CAVE!

Then one day they climbed a mountain to the top of the world!

"Oh, Crab!" exclaimed Dog. "I never knew there was so much to see."

They met others on their own journeys too.

"I used to be scared of heights," Mouse smiled. "But look at me now - right up here!"

"Only if you say it is," chuckled Dog. And together, they had the tent up in no time!

That night Dog and Crab were warm and snug as the wind howled around them.

"And I always got in a flap," said Flamingo. "But now I can do anything. Except put up tents on windy mountains. That's IMPOSSIBLE!"

By morning all was calm . . .

. . . but the road to the ocean was blocked!

Dog and Crab had come so far.
"We can move that tree, can't we, Crab?" asked Dog.
"We'll finish our journey, won't we?"

But Crab knew that this time
it really was impossible.
"Dog, the thing is," he began,
when . . .

VROOOOM!
It was Flamingo in her monster truck.
"Let's get this tree shifted!" she called.

Soon Dog and Crab were on their way again.
"Follow that seaside breeze!" said Crab.
So they did just that, on and on until . . .

"The ocean!" whooped Dog.
"Home!" cheered Crab. "We did it,
Dog – we DID it!"

At last, it was time to explore . . .

Dog flew kites, he jumped waves,
he built castles in the sand.

And the pale blue fish that once
flickered from his nightlight
now swam around him in all the
colours of the rainbow!

How Dog wished he
could stay forever.
But every holiday
has to end.

"I must go back," he sighed,
"to my job and my home."
"But you love it here!" cried Crab.

Dog nodded. "But to stay is imposs—"
Then he stopped.
"It's only impossible if I SAY it is . . ." gasped Dog.

On the sunniest beach, by the
calmest ocean, Dog and Crab now
run the most magical café.
And together, NOTHING feels impossible!